Disney · PIXAR

Cars

5-MINUTE RACING STORIES

DISNEP PRESS
Los Angeles • New York

CONTENTS

PIT CREW TO THE RESCUE   1

REVVED UP IN RADIATOR SPRINGS   15

CRASH COURSE   29

DUSTUP IN THE DESERT   45

FAME IN THE FAST LANE   61

RAMMIN' SLAMMIN' RELAY   77

REMATCH   91

NEON RACERS   107

ICE RACERS   119

RALLY TO THE FINISH!   135

RACING FOR GOOD   153

A NEW RACER   169

PIT CREW TO THE RESCUE!

It had been an exciting afternoon in Radiator Springs. Lightning McQueen was on TV, talking about the big Piston Cup tiebreaker race.

"Do you think he can beat Chick Hicks?" Sally asked.

"Lightning can beat anybody!" said Mater excitedly.

"We should head on out there to cheer him on. He needs us," Doc said.

"Whoo-ee! A road trip!" Mater shouted.

The road to California was long. To keep from getting tired, the cars stopped at several rest stops.

"Hey, look," Mater called out as he peered over the edge of a cliff. "That town is just like Radiator Springs."

"There's only one Radiator Springs," Doc said. "But I *do* think you've found us a shortcut." Mater beamed. Then he realized that Guido was missing. Worried, Mater went to look for the little forklift.

Mater found Guido at the end of the line of cars. It was hot, and little Guido had fallen way behind.

A frantic Luigi begged Mater, "Please help Guido!"

Doing a tight U-turn, Mater spun around and hooked the weary forklift onto his tow cable. Mater was going to give Guido a lift to California!

"I hope you don't mind lookin' at where we've been instead of where we're going," Mater said.

Finally, the Radiator Springs gang arrived at the Los Angeles International Speedway. It was almost race time!

Sarge took command. "Flo, oil stand over here. Guido, tires and tools right there."

"Pit stop!" Guido shouted. Shaking with excitement, he went to work.

Ramone was itching to do some painting.

Doc had a suggestion. "Try snazzing up this pit. We need to show off our star car."

"Where *is* Lightning?" Mater wondered.

"Come on, Mater," Doc said. "Let's find the kid."

There were so many cars around that Doc and Mater had trouble
spotting Lightning.

"There he is!" Mater shouted.

Doc turned to look, but Lightning was already gone.

Determined to find his friend, Mater began a search of his own.
"Lightning McQueen!" Mater shouted. "Where you at, buddy?"

Just then, Mater spotted the tent for Rust-eze, Lightning's racing
sponsor. Maybe his friend was in there.

Inside, Mater found himself surrounded by rusty cars.

"Hey, you're Lightning's pal Tow Mater!" said an old van.

"How about a free sample, Mater?" said a grinning blue car. "It will take some of that rust off your bumper."

"Rust? On me? Where?" Mater asked, alarmed.

Suddenly, Flo rushed in and took Mater away.

"Come back soon!" the rusty cars called.

Mater and Flo went in search of decorations for Lightning's pit area. They found a truck that was selling lots of cool stuff. Mater picked out some snazzy antenna balls.

"Oh, I like those," Flo said, and then added some yellow banners that matched Lightning's team colors.

"Looks like we're going to have a ball today," said Mater with a grin.

"Good one, Mater," said Flo, laughing.

Doc was checking out the other crews when he heard Chick Hicks say, "I'm winning this time, no matter *what* I have to do. I'm going to force The King and that smart-alecky rookie off the track. The cup is mine, boys."

Doc knew he had to warn Lightning that Chick was up to his usual dirty tricks. But where *was* Lightning?

Doc found Mater and told him about Chick's plan.

"We gotta warn Lightning!" Mater yelled.

"I think I saw Mack over there," Doc said. "We've got to get closer. If we find Mack, we'll find Lightning."

"This area is for press only," said a tough-looking SUV guard.

It looked like Doc wasn't going to get to Lightning in time. "Sorry to let you down, kid," he said quietly.

Mater didn't like seeing Doc look so sad and defeated. "Here, Doc, this is for you," he said, tossing Doc one of the antenna balls. "It has Lightning's number on it, so you won't forget—we're part of his team."

Doc grinned. "You're right, Mater. We came here to help our friend, and that's exactly what we're going to do!"

Mater spun around and let out a holler. "Whoo-ee! Here we come, Lightning!" he yelled.

"Let's get to the pit," said Doc. "And tell Ramone I need a special paint job!"

As he made a turn around the track, Lightning McQueen saw his Radiator Springs friends in the pit crew area. They had come all the way to California to cheer him on!

"Hey kid, keep an eye on Hicks," Doc said over his radio headset. "He's up to no good."

Lightning wasn't worried. He knew that Doc and Mater and all his friends were looking out for him.

Newly energized, Lightning gunned his motor and took off down the racetrack. *Ka-chow!*

REVVED UP IN RADIATOR SPRINGS

Life in Radiator Springs was about to change forever. "Doc and I want to build a racing headquarters near the town," Lightning McQueen told Sally.

Doc Hudson nodded. "It will be a special design—a first-class track that won't spoil our beautiful desert landscape."

"That's a great idea!" said Sally. "The new track will put Radiator Springs back on the map."

Soon Radiator Springs was the talk of the racing world. For the grand opening race, Lightning and Doc sent invitations to race cars everywhere.

Lightning was looking forward to racing against two famous cars from Europe: Otto from Germany and Gudmund from Sweden. They were both cool, superfast cars!

Soon, race cars began to arrive from all over.

The cars from Europe drove really fast! An outraged Sheriff kept giving out speeding tickets, but the cars did not understand.

Otto, the silver car from Germany, kept rolling his front tire over the speeding ticket. He thought Sheriff was asking for his autograph!

In town, Otto tried to ask Lizzie for directions to the stadium. But Lizzie didn't understand. She thought Otto wanted to purchase her deluxe Radiator Springs sticker set.

Soon Otto was covered in bumper stickers!

Lightning couldn't help laughing at a sticker-covered Otto. He led the race car to Ramone's body shop for a fresh paint job.

As they drove away, Lizzie tooted her horn.

As the time for the race approached, Lightning and his friends decided to take a look at the new stadium.

"Wait, Lightning," Sheriff said, driving up alongside him. "Gudmund isn't here. I'm worried he might be lost."

Lightning was worried, too. "Let's form a search party," he said.

Mater offered to help, too. "As long as we don't have to go into any caves!" he said.

Lightning, Sheriff, and Mater searched all day and into the night. They couldn't find Gudmund anywhere. There was just one last place to look: the caves.

"You want to go in there?" Mater asked, his voice shaking.

"We don't have time to be scared," Sheriff said. "We have to find Gudmund."

Bravely, Sheriff led Lightning and Mater into the dark cave.

The three cars pulled into the cavern. Suddenly, they saw flickering lights up ahead.

"What'd ya do with Gudmund, you no-good ghost?" shouted Mater, trying to hide behind Lightning.

"That's no ghost," exclaimed Lightning. "It's Gudmund!"

Gudmund was an explorer. He had roof lights that were perfect for mountain roads and caves. He wasn't lost. He was just exploring the caverns around Radiator Springs!

"Hey, Lightning!" said Gudmund. "Driving in here is a blast! Wanna join me?"

"You bet!" answered Lightning as he revved his engine.

Since Lightning didn't have headlights, Sheriff set him up with night-vision goggles. As Lightning and Gudmund raced through the caves together, Mater stayed outside.

"If you fellas need anything, just honk your horns . . . and I'll send in Sheriff."

The next morning, all the race cars showed up for the first Radiator Springs International Invitational. Before the crowds arrived, the cars met to go over the rules and to welcome their special announcer: Mater!

"Check, one-two-four," said Mater. "Is this thing on?" He tapped the microphone. Then it started to screech.

"Oooh, my ears!" said Sally. "Maybe we should have asked Bob Cutlass to announce. He's a professional."

"That may be so," said Doc as he headed down to the pit. "But nobody can replace our Mater. He'll do just fine."

Mater was a great announcer! "And they're off," he said excitedly into the microphone. "Otto from Germany is neck and neck with our very own Lightning McQueen!"

The crowd cheered as the cars whipped around the track.

"I've never seen Lightning race so hard," said Sally.

"He's never raced against a car like Otto," Doc said. "I hope Lightning doesn't wear himself out too fast."

Lightning and Otto were both worn out! They had raced hard and they were running out of steam.

Lightning looked out at the stands and saw Mater, Doc, Sally, and his other friends. They were so excited. This was the first race in their new stadium!

Lightning knew he had to dig deeper. He had to win this one for Radiator Springs.

In the home stretch, Lightning heard his friend Mater call to him over the loudspeaker: "Come on, buddy, you can do it!"

Grinning, Lightning gunned his engine. "This one's for you, Mater," he hollered. Then he sped across the finish line—tongue first!

After the race, Lightning invited Otto and Gudmund to stay in town for a while. "There's more to Radiator Springs than racing," he said. "Around here, fun and friendship mean way more than trophies!"

Disney · PIXAR

Cars

CRASH COURSE

Lightning McQueen zoomed around Radiator Springs Speedway, the town's fancy new racetrack. These days the race car spent most of his time teaching at the newly opened Fabulous Hudson Hornet Academy. But between classes, Lightning loved driving laps.

"Is that the best you can do, kid?" asked Doc Hudson.

Before Lightning could answer, Mater pulled up from behind. He was gleefully driving backward. "Better watch out! I'm right on yer tail!" he yelled.

Not far away, Chick Hicks was running his own academy—for sly, sneaky cars!

Chick liked to show off in front of his students. He dazzled them with his special style of racing, also known as the Three Cs—cheat, cheat, and cheat.

Chick's star student was a devious steel-gray car named Switcher. Chick had taught him everything he knew.

Both racing academies wanted to prove they were the best. So everyone was excited when the Race-O-Rama competition was announced. The competition had four races in four different locations. Racers from academies all over the country would be participating. But Lightning knew the real competition would be between Doc's and Chick's schools.

"This will be great publicity for the academy," said Doc.

"Especially when we beat Chick," Lightning added.

The first race was a head-to-head battle, two cars versus two cars. When Chick learned that Lightning and Mater would be a team, he couldn't wait to sign up with Switcher.

Chick wanted to make sure he'd race to victory. So he got a bigger engine—to match his massive mean streak. He also trained Switcher daily, making sure his star student was in prime shape to be his partner in the race.

"You call that speed?" Chick yelled. "My Grandma Hicks can drive faster than you!"

Switcher narrowed his eyes and accelerated, hitting 150 miles per hour in no time.

The day of the race soon arrived. Excitement filled the air at
Radiator Springs Speedway.

Mater, Lightning, Chick, and Switcher approached the starting
line. Switcher looked at Lightning and Mater. "That's our
competition?" he said loudly to Chick. "I could beat them with
my eyes closed."

"Oh, you'll have your eyes closed, because you'll be crying
when I leave you in the dust!" said Lightning.

Before Switcher could respond, the green flag waved and the race began! The cars took off. They each had to complete one hundred laps!

Lightning immediately took the lead, but Switcher and Chick were on his bumper. In fact, Chick rammed right into the back of Lightning!

"Get out of my way," Chick growled.

"Gladly," replied Lightning, smiling. Firing up his new turbo boost, he whooshed ahead.

Chick snarled. "Go get him!" he told Switcher.

Switcher grinned wickedly. "With pleasure."

Using his own turbo boost, Switcher caught up to Lightning.

"What took you so long?" Lightning joked.

Switcher wasn't in the mood to laugh. He was, however, in the mood to cheat. Pulling ahead of Lightning, Switcher released a stream of oil behind him. Lightning's tires skidded through the oil. He slid uncontrollably down the racetrack and was forced to slam on his brakes.

Chick pulled alongside Switcher. "Did you see that? No one can stop me," Switcher boasted. "See you at the finish line!" And with that, he sped ahead of Chick.

Chick's eyes narrowed. He'd had enough of Switcher's attitude. "If that tin can thinks he's taking first place, he's in for a surprise."

BAM! Chick rammed right into Switcher. "It's time you learned your place," he said.

Switcher flipped over the track. He finally came to a stop in the infield, smoke pouring from his hood.

"I'm on *your* team!" he yelled.

"Not anymore!" Chick replied, accelerating.

Lightning and Mater pulled into the pit area. Guido, Sarge, and Luigi changed their tires and filled up the cars with gas.

"I can't believe Chick did that to his own teammate," Lightning said. "I think it's time to give him a taste of his own fuel."

"You mean like Chick's Three Cs?" said Doc.

"No, I think it's time to put our own Plan C into action," Lightning answered.

"What's Plan C?" asked Mater.

"No time to explain," Doc said. "Just follow my instructions."

After the pit stop, the cars roared back
onto the track. There were only five laps left.

Immediately, Doc gave Mater the instructions he
needed.

Mater began weaving back and forth in front of Chick. Every time
Chick tried to get ahead, Mater blocked his path.

"Stop it, you hunk of junk!" Chick yelled.

"Aw, shucks, flattery will get you nowhere," said Mater with a smile.

Doc instructed Lightning to move forward on the inside track.
Lightning raced across the finish line!

"*Noooo!*" yelled Chick.

On the award podium, Doc congratulated Lightning and Mater on winning the Silver Tailfin Trophy. "Great job, team," said Doc. "Plan C worked really well."

"What's the C stand for?" asked Mater.

"Cooperation," Doc explained. "Fancy gadgets and upgrades are great, but they can't compete against good old cooperation."

"And it's way better than Chick's Three Cs!" Lightning said.

Doc, Mater, and Lightning smiled for the cameras. Their first Race-O-Rama win felt great!

DUSTUP IN THE DESERT

El Machismo raced across the dry lake bed in the canyon. The rocks he went over didn't bother him at all. It was what he was used to. It was what he was built for.

"Oh, yeeeeaaaaah!" the truck yelled gleefully, enjoying every bump and bounce.

Watching from above, Chick Hicks kept a close eye on his prized student. "El Machismo is going to crush Lightning McQueen at Autovia!" he said with a smile.

Autovia was a supertough desert track. El Machismo and Chick would be racing against Lightning and his partner. The problem was, the race was just a few days away, and Doc hadn't found a teammate for Lightning. None of his students had experience with harsh terrain.

Sarge was driving by and stopped to watch his friends practice. "Don't you know how to hill climb?" he yelled. "What if you get stuck in a silt bed?"

Lightning pulled alongside the 4x4. "Hey, Sarge! If you know so much about desert terrain, why don't you race with me?"

Sarge was stunned. "I've never raced before," he said.

"How about I teach you how to race, and you teach me all about driving off-road?" Lightning suggested.

"All right, soldier," Sarge agreed. "That sounds like a plan."

Training started at dawn the next morning, in a nearby canyon.

"Drop and give me twenty-five miles! Go!" Sarge barked.

Doing twenty-five miles was no problem for Lightning. Doing it on rocky terrain was a different story. "Ow, ow, ow!" he said as he bumped along.

"You need better tires, soldier!" yelled Sarge. "This isn't a stadium!"

Lightning taught Sarge that racing against
Chick Hicks took some special maneuvers. "Chick Hicks doesn't play
fair, so the plan is to be prepared for the unexpected," Lightning
explained. He put Sarge through an obstacle course full
of surprises.

Sarge saved his most important lesson for last. "To win this race, you have to know how to handle one thing: silt."

Lightning frowned. "Silt? You mean the dusty dirt in old lake beds? That's the big important lesson?"

Sarge looked at Lightning. "Listen up, soldier. Make sure you're in the lead before the course goes into the silt beds. Then keep pushing the gas. If you don't, you'll get stuck. It's impossible to see through, and you'll want to stop. Don't. Just keep going."

"Yes, sir!" Lightning replied.

Finally, race day arrived. Both Lightning and Chick had new modifications, including fog lights and all-terrain tires.

"Bow down to the tower of power!" El Machismo called to the crowd. "Oh, yeeeeaaaaah!"

"I think it's time that oversized hcap of metal learned how to lose gracefully," Sarge said.

Sarge and Chick would be racing first.

"Get ready to lose, old man," Chick said to Sarge, gunning his motor.

"Get ready to wave your white flag of surrender!" replied Sarge, narrowing his eyes.

Soon the green flag waved, and the race began!

About a quarter of the way through the race, Chick sped in front of Sarge and released a bunch of bolts on the ground behind him.

Sarge remembered what Lightning had taught him. He veered off the path to avoid the bolts and swiftly handled the rocky terrain. Then he headed to the pit stop.

Chick was too busy looking at what Sarge was doing to watch where he was going. *CRASH!* He collided with a giant cactus!

Covered with needles, Chick limped to the pit stop, where El Machismo was waiting. "You make sure you beat that Lightning McQueen," he said sternly. "We can't lose this race."

"No problem," El Machismo said. "Wait till I get him on the dirt. I'll shred him like paper!"

Chick was pleased. But just in case, he had a backup plan. To guarantee Lightning wouldn't even finish the race, Chick intended to move the course marker. Lightning would be headed off course without even knowing it!

El Machismo and Lightning zoomed across the desert plains, around tight corners, and over a rickety bridge. When El Machismo jumped a hill, there was so much space between him and the ground that it looked like he was flying.

Uh-oh, thought Lightning. *This guy is tougher than I thought.*

Lightning remembered that he needed to be in front before he hit the silt beds. Just as the path narrowed, he pulled into the lead. When he reached the silt beds, clouds of dusty sand exploded all around him.

Lightning kept moving forward, pushing through the heavy silt. He couldn't see a thing, but he didn't dare stop. After one last push, Lightning finally made it out.

"Now that's what I call off-road racing!" he exclaimed.

The dust from the silt beds rained down on Chick, who was hiding nearby. He was blinded by the dust, but he heard a car race by. He used his windshield wipers to clear his view and then hurried to move the course marker before the next car came through.

"This will teach that hotshot to mess with Chick Hicks," he said. "Let's see how he likes a detour!"

As Lightning neared the finish line, he looked around for El Machismo. To his surprise, the truck was nowhere in sight!

Lightning crossed the finish line. "Ka-chow!" he shouted.

"Wait!" Chick yelled. "You were supposed to take the detour!"

The race officials didn't like the sound of that and took Chick in for questioning.

Lightning and Sarge were awarded the Silver Tailfin Trophy. "Congratulations on winning your first race," Lightning told Sarge. "Thanks, soldier. We make a pretty good team!" Sarge replied.

Meanwhile, El Machismo, who had accidentally taken the detour meant for Lightning, finally found his way to the finish line. "What? I lost?" he yelled. "Oh, noooooooo!"

FAME IN THE FAST LANE

"I could get used to this!" Lightning McQueen said. He and Sally had just arrived in sunny Santa Carburera for the latest event in the Race-O-Rama series. There were swaying palm trees, spectacular beaches, and more than a few celebrities.

"Why don't we check out some of the hot spots?" Lightning suggested.

"There'll be plenty of time for that later," replied Sally. "Right now you need to focus on winning tomorrow's race!"

Lightning was going to represent the Fabulous Hudson Hornet Academy. He'd be up against a student from Chick Hicks's racing school—but so far Chick was keeping the car's identity top secret.

"Don't worry," Lightning said as he and Sally arrived at the racetrack. "Whoever my opponent is, he doesn't stand a chance."

"Better make that *she*," Sally replied.

Lightning looked up. Chick was cruising toward him with a gleaming pink car by his side!

Suddenly, fans appeared out of nowhere and surrounded the pink car. "Meet Candice—racing's hottest new celebrity," Chick said.

Lightning was speechless. He had been gearing up to race against a mean muscle car or a rough-and-tough truck. A shiny pink car was the last thing he expected.

"No need to say a word," Candice said. "Fans often get tongue-tied around me. Now, if you'll excuse me, I have a photo shoot!"

"What a show-off!" Sally said.

But Lightning wasn't bothered. "I've seen her kind before," he replied. "You know, the type of car who wants the glory with none of the hard work."

"Speaking of hard work," Sally said, "you should have started practicing by now. No more talking! Let's get moving!"

"Yes, ma'am!" replied Lightning—then burst out laughing.

"What?" Sally asked.

Lightning smiled. "I think you've been hanging around Sarge too long!"

That night, after Lightning fell asleep, Sally cruised the race grounds. When she got to Candice's tent, she saw a lively party taking place inside.

"Are you sure you're ready for the race?" Sally overheard Chick Hicks ask.

"Of course," Candice snapped. "I've got a few tricks even you haven't seen yet."

The next morning, Sally joined Lightning for some last-minute practice turns. "Just ease into it and let yourself drift," Sally suggested.

Soon Lightning was turning like an expert—but Sally looked concerned. "What's the matter?" he asked.

Sally told him what Candice had said the night before.

"If she has to resort to tricks, then I guess she doesn't have that much confidence in her skills," Lightning declared. "Fortunately, I have plenty in mine."

When Lightning pulled up to the starting line, Candice was posing for the cameras.

"Lightning, please!" she said. "You're blocking my good side!"

"You know, Candice," Lightning said, "Doc Hudson taught me there's a lot more to racing than fame."

"Like what?" Candice asked.

"Well, things like skill, sportsmanship . . ." Lightning began.

But Candice wasn't listening. She was too busy soaking up the limelight!

The starting flag went down, and Lightning and Candice sped off. Lightning quickly took the lead, but he didn't hold it for long.

At the first turn, Candice used a drifting maneuver that allowed her to coast right in front of him. When Lightning tried to pass her, she tilted her body toward the sun. The sunlight reflected off her ultrashiny paint and into Lightning's eyes. He couldn't see where he was going, and he drove right off the track!

Lightning rejoined the race and tried to overtake Candice, but she pushed him onto the shoulder. The next time he came up beside her, she used the sun to blind him again.

Watching from the sidelines, Sally knew she had to do something. "Lightning!" she called. "Hang back so Candice thinks she's won for sure, then zoom up and use the drifting move we practiced this morning. Once you're out in front, floor it to the finish line!"

Lightning took Sally's advice—and the lead!

"Hey, Candice!" Chick Hicks screamed. "Losers don't make the front page! You'd better win this thing!"

Candice sped ahead of Lightning, then swerved over to some dunes and spewed sand at Lightning as he passed her.

"This better be worth it!" whined Candice. "I hate getting sand in my tires!"

While Lightning stopped to clear the sand from his eyes, Candice smiled. Her trick had worked!

"Hey, Candice! How about looking this way?" shouted a photographer.

Candice turned, triggering a dozen cameras. She blinked frantically, trying to recover from the blinding flashes.

At the same moment, Lightning raced ahead and crossed the finish line!

"And Lightning McQueen wins it!" shouted the announcer.

"I don't believe it!" wailed Chick Hicks. "How could this happen?"

Lightning proudly received his Silver Tailfin Trophy.

"Ka-chow!" he said as he smiled for the cameras.

Finally, it was time to sightsee and have some fun. Being in the spotlight was fine, but being with Sally was even better!

RAMMIN' SLAMMIN' RELAY

"Whoa! Flashy!" Ramone exclaimed, looking at the bright neon lights of Motoropolis City.

"This place is amazing," Lightning said. "I love the challenge of racing in a city. I just know we can win this!"

Lightning and Ramone were representing the Fabulous Hudson Hornet Academy in a relay race. They were going up against Chick Hicks and a student from his racing school named Stinger.

"I know what will help us win," said Ramone. He took Lightning to a body shop he had set up in a tent. "Check it out! A glow-in-the-dark paint job! Decked out in this, we'll *really* be able to see tonight."

Lightning knew there were lights all over the city to show them the way. But he didn't want to dampen Ramone's enthusiasm. "Okay," he said. "Paint me up, Ramone!"

Meanwhile, across town, Chick Hicks was working on his team's strategy. They were going to cheat—but he warned Stinger not to let the judges catch them, or they'd be disqualified.

"And I don't want you to take Lightning out of just this race," Chick barked as Stinger practiced his famous ramming move. "I want you to take him out for good!"

That night, the air in Motoropolis City was filled with excitement.

Ramone and Chick cruised to the starting line for the first leg of the relay. When they reached Brakeaway Tunnel, they would tag their partners. Then Lightning and Stinger would race the second leg to the finish line.

An official waved the starting flag. They were off!

Chick immediately crowded Ramone toward a building. But Ramone used his super hydraulics to lift himself high above the race car. Chick slid underneath Ramone and—SMASH!—hit the brick himself!

As Ramone took the lead, Stinger appeared and dumped a load of bolts in the road. He wasn't even supposed to be in the race yet! *Four flats, coming up,* Chick thought.

But Ramone's heavy-duty tires sailed right over the mess. Chick wasn't so lucky. He hit every single bolt.

"I've got to make a pit stop," Chick told Stinger angrily. "Do whatever it takes to slow him down!"

A little while later, Ramone saw a roadblock ahead and screeched to a stop. Stinger had struck again!

Ramone had no choice but to detour off into a maze of
one-way streets. Soon he was hopelessly lost.

Then, a miracle! Ramone glanced down a long street—
and saw Brakeaway Tunnel in the distance. He hit the gas.

"Hang on, Lightning," he cried. "I'm coming!"

Suddenly, Chick zoomed up next to Ramone and pushed him against a warehouse. Ramone had nowhere to go but up the ramp to the building's loading dock. Thinking quickly, he launched himself off. "I love to drive," shouted Ramone. "But when you're short on time, flying is the only way to go!"

Chick had accidentally helped Ramone get even closer to the relay point!

Ramone floored it while Chick blasted out of the side street. Both cars reached Brakeaway Tunnel and tagged their partners at exactly the same time!

Lightning was a blur as he entered the tunnel just before Stinger. Seconds later —thanks to Chick—the lights went out. Lightning had to slow down. Without headlights, he couldn't see a thing. Then his eyes adjusted. His new paint job was casting a glow inside the tunnel!

"Thank you, Ramone!" Lightning cried.

Stinger was on Lightning's tail. As they exited the tunnel, he accelerated and rammed into his opponent. Lightning skidded into a big pothole—and couldn't get out!

"Lucky hit!" Lightning yelled. "I'd like to see you do that again!"

BAM! Stinger hit Lightning so hard that he lurched right out of the hole.

"Thanks!" Lightning called as he took the lead again. "I couldn't have done it without you!"

Chick was watching from the sidelines. "I don't care what you have to do—just cross that finish line first!" he yelled at Stinger.

Stinger knew what that meant. He left the road and took a shortcut through a parking lot.

POP! POP! POP! POP!

All four of his tires went flat!

Meanwhile, Lightning crossed the finish line to the cheers of his fans. "Ka-chow!" he exclaimed as he posed for the cameras. "The best racing school in the world wins again!"

A little while later, Lightning and Ramone proudly accepted their Silver Tailfin Trophy.

"Lightning," said a reporter, "do you have any words of advice for Chick and Stinger?"

"Yeah," Lightning said. "Racing the wrong way is never the right thing to do!"

REMATCH

*F*rancesco Bernoulli had challenged Lightning to a race in his hometown: Monza, Italy.

"Benvenuto!" Francesco said when Lightning arrived. "Your plane was late, but this is no surprise. You will be late crossing the finish line, too."

Lightning smiled. Then he turned to his best friend, Mater. "I am so beating him—right here on his own turf!" he whispered.

As the racers left the runway, they were surrounded by photographers. Francesco showed off his right side. He showed off his left side.

"Everyone loves Francesco. He has many fans," he told Lightning.

"Nobody has more fans than Lightning!" Mater piped up.

Francesco rolled his eyes.

"We will prove it!" said Luigi. "Lightning gets hundreds of fan letters each day. Guido, bring the mailbag!"

Guido zoomed off! He returned a few minutes later with mailbags overflowing with fan letters.

Lightning was a little embarrassed. "Oh, it's really not that big of a deal," he said. "It's just a few letters from my fans."

"You are right, Lightning," said Francesco. "It is no big deal, because Francesco has much, much more fan mail! You see. Everyone loves Francesco!"

"Letters are great," said Lightning. "But we like to get some fender-to-fender time with our fans whenever we can."

Lightning turned and wheeled through the doors to the airport. Outside was a line of fans, just waiting to see him.

Lightning greeted the cars. He even stopped to take a picture with each one. Meanwhile, Mater got the fans going. They began chanting: "Light-*ning*! Light-*ning*!"

"*Questo è ridicolo!*" mumbled Francesco. "And what about autographs?" he asked. "Watch—and be amazed."

Francesco started spinning his wheels. Hundreds of autographed photos of himself flew behind him, onto the windshields of his waiting fans.

"See? Francesco always gets things done at three hundred kilometers an hour."

After the two racers finished greeting their fans, they drove to a café. "Hey, Mr. Francesco, nobody drinks oil faster than Lightning," said Mater.

"What?" said Lightning. "Mater, I can't drink—"

"C'mon, buddy, show 'em what I done taught you!" said Mater.

Lightning sighed and managed to finish a can of oil in a few gulps.

Francesco was not impressed. "Francesco never guzzles," he said. "Oil should be savored."

Lightning cruised over to Francesco. "How about a warm-up before the big race—just you and me?" he asked.

Francesco nodded. "Ah, good idea, Lightning! Try to keep up, if you . . ."

Before Francesco could finish, Lightning was a red streak down the road!

"Ka-*ciao*, Francesco!" yelled Lightning.

Francesco had almost caught up with Lightning when he nearly spun out on a left turn.

"How do you make those left turns so well?" Francesco asked.

"Get equipped with some treaded tires," said Lightning. "Then turn right to go left. A very good friend taught me that once."

Soon the race cars stopped to rest. Francesco sighed. "Ahh, Italia is beautiful, no? Just like Francesco!"

Lightning chuckled. "Do you always think about yourself?" he asked.

"Of course," said Francesco. "On the racetrack, Francesco only thinks about himself and doing his best. This is why he always wins!"

The next day was the big race. Finally, the world would find out who was the fastest race car!

When the flag dropped, the fans went wild!

Francesco came out of the first left turn ahead of Lightning. He showed off his new treaded tires. "Perhaps Lightning has taught Francesco too well!"

As Lightning zoomed into the Monza arena, he got distracted by the camera flashes and the screaming fans. Suddenly, he remembered what Francesco had said.

Lightning looked straight ahead. He blocked out the photographers and the fans, focused on his performance, and quickly took the lead!

As the two cars crossed the finish line, the crowd gasped.

"Ka-chow!" yelled Lightning. "I won!"

"You mean *ciao bella*," said Francesco. "Francesco won!"

The truth stunned everyone. According to the judges, the race was a *tie*!

That evening, the cars tried to figure out what to do. How could they award a trophy when there had been no winner?

Then Francesco shouted, "No more talk! Talk is slow. What do we do? We race!"

"That's a great idea!" said Lightning. "We'll race in Radiator Springs!"

Then the two fastest cars in the world zoomed away together . . . to race again another day.

NEON RACERS

Lightning McQueen was competing in the Transcontinental Race of Champions—T-ROC—a series of races hosted by his international racing friends. Shu Todoroki was hosting the first race in Japan.

"*Buona sera*, Lightning!" said Francesco, an Italian racer. "Francesco is looking forward to beating you in Tokyo."

"Then I'm afraid Francesco will be very disappointed . . . especially when he sees this!" Lightning spun around and showed off a SAYONARA FRANCESCO bumper sticker.

Just then, another car drove up. It was Carla Veloso, the racer from Brazil. "You boys are so wrapped up in your own rivalry, you won't even notice when I speed right past you," she said.

Before Lightning or Francesco could respond, a white car cruised up to the racers. It was Shu's crew chief, Mach Matsuo. "Welcome to Japan," he said. "Shu is waiting for you at our racing headquarters. If you'll follow me, I'll show you the way. . . ."

At his headquarters, Shu explained the race. "We'll be racing at night—an eighty-five-mile trip from Mount Fuji to Ginza."

Shu motioned for several of his pit crew members to come forward. "Since we'll be racing in the dark, we'll need special competition lighting."

Shu darkened his race shop. The other racers gasped. The Japanese race car was glowing!

The next evening, the racers—all lit up in bright neon—met at
Base Camp Five, halfway up Mount Fuji.

"Welcome, racers," Shu said. "When the flag drops, you may head
straight down the mountain. But, for those who would like to join the
ranks of Mount Fuji's most legendary racers, you may head up . . . and
sign the climbers' book at the top of the mountain!"

"That climb looks intense," a racer named Rip said. "You can count me out. It's straight to Ginza for me."

"Francesco agrees with Rip," said the formula car. "Francesco will win the race and then sign autographs!"

"The choice is yours," said Shu. "*Ganbatte minna-san!* Good luck, everyone!"

The flag dropped and the cars took off! Francesco and most of the other racers headed down the mountain. But Lightning wasn't about to take the easy way out. He wanted the honor of signing the climbers' book!

Lightning, Shu, Carla, Lewis Hamilton, and Vitaly Petrov drove up the rugged terrain, hugging the curves and skidding across patches of ice on their way to the top of the mountain.

"There it is!" Shu called out when the racers reached the summit. "The climbers' book!"

"Ka-chow!" Lightning cried, signing the book. The other racers followed suit.

As the racers turned to head back down the mountain, Shu stopped them. "I forgot to mention the other reward for reaching the peak of Mount Fuji: there's a road that leads straight down! Follow me!"

"Now you're talkin'!" yelled Lightning.

The five racers flew down the mountain. Suddenly, their road merged with another. The racers spotted the other cars just ahead of them. They had caught up with the racers who had taken the easier path!

"Let's show them what neon speed really looks like!" yelled Lightning.

The racers sped up, their lights glowing brightly. They looked like streaks of red, gold, green, blue, and white in the night.

Soon Lightning caught up to Francesco.

"Lightning McQueen! Where did you come from?" asked Francesco in shock.

"You didn't think I'd make it easy on you, did you, Francesco?" Lightning asked. Then, smiling and revving his engine, he took the lead!

Finally, the racers entered Tokyo's colorful Ginza district. As the cars neared the finish line, Francesco edged out a lead. But with a burst of speed, Lightning cut in front of him!

The two racers were so focused on passing each other, they didn't notice a car behind them. It was Carla Veloso! As promised, she slipped by the two competitors and won the race!

On the winner's podium, Shu presented Carla with the Neon Racers Cup trophy.

"Neon racing was amazing! Thanks for hosting, Shu," said Lightning. Then he turned to this friends. "So . . . where to next?"

ICE RACERS

"Welcome to Moscow!" exclaimed Vitaly Petrov. The Russian racer was hosting the next leg of the Transcontinental Race of Champions—T-ROC. "Moscow is amazing, Vitaly!" said Lightning McQueen.

"If you think the city is beautiful, wait until you see the countryside," Vitaly said. "We'll be ice racing there tomorrow."

The next morning, the racers gathered in Vitaly's headquarters. A major snowstorm had passed through Moscow overnight. It was all anyone could talk about!

Carla Veloso, the racer from Brazil, peered out a window. "There's nearly a meter of snow on the ground!" she said.

"That's in the city," added Lightning. "The conditions will be even worse in the countryside."

"Don't worry, everyone. I will find a solution!" said Vitaly.

Vitaly quickly plotted a new race course through the city. "We can race on the closed roads with our studded tires," he said.

Soon the racers were ready to go. They pulled up to the starting line at Saint Battery's Cathedral.

"Is everyone ready to ice race?" Vitaly called out.

The racers answered by revving their engines.

"Let's put these tires to the test!" Lightning yelled.

The racers zoomed away, leaving a cloud of snow behind them.

Soon the racers passed the historic Balljoint Theater. "The most beautiful ballet and opera performances in the world are held at the Balljoint," Vitaly called back to his friends.

Shu Todoroki, the Japanese racer, couldn't help smiling at the Russian racer. "Not only does he make this look easy, he's giving us a tour at the same time!"

Just as the racers completed the first circle around the city, they encountered a roadblock. "It's no problem! Follow me!" Vitaly shouted. He sped down a ramp and into an underground metro station. The racers admired the graceful archways and the marble floors. But most of all, they appreciated the warmth!

As the racers emerged from the station, they were caught off guard by a truck carrying huge bales of hay. The hay was covering the truck's eyes so he couldn't see the oncoming racers!

Vitaly, Raoul ÇaRoule, Lightning, Francesco Bernoulli, and Max Schnell quickly swerved around the truck. But Rip Clutchgoneski couldn't make it. He turned too quickly and spun out!

Vitaly looked back to make sure Rip was okay.

"I'm fine!" Rip yelled out to his friends as he came to a stop on the side of the road. "Don't worry, I'll catch up!"

When the racers reached the bank of the frozen Moscow River, Vitaly presented them with an option.

"Since there might be more hazards on the road ahead, you may want to take a detour along the river."

Some of the racers looked concerned.

"The choice is yours," Vitaly said.

Five of the racers decided to stick to the road, while the other seven decided to take the river route. They would all meet up at the Central Moscow Hybridrome, where they would complete three laps before crossing the finish line.

Vitaly gave the river racers a few words of advice. "Stay close to the bank, where the ice is more solid. If you are going too fast, ease off the gas and let your studded tires do the work."

The seven racers on the river skimmed the ice with ease. Lightning couldn't believe how fast he was going.

"This must be what flying feels like!" he said, relishing a blast of cold wind against his face.

Back on the main road, Shu, Nigel
Gearsley, Rip, Miguel Camino, and Carla
were regretting their decision. They were at
a standstill on a bridge as they waited for a
snowplow to clear the road.

Just then they heard a voice from the river
below. It was Vitaly.

"Hello, comrades! Everything okay up there?"
he called.

The cars on the bridge sighed heavily.

Down below, the river racers were facing problems of their own. Max's tire had cracked through the ice!

"Keep going without me," said Max.

"No! Never leave a comrade behind. There's more to this race than just winning," Vitaly said.

Jeff Gorvette drove up. "Let me stay with Max. You need to guide the others down the river."

Vitaly agreed and thanked Jeff. Then he called out to the others, "Stay the course! Onward toward the Hybridrome!"

Even though the river route was longer than the road course, the river racers were the first to arrive at the Hybridrome! As they began their laps around the stadium, several racing fans showed up to cheer them on.

Shu, Nigel, Miguel, Carla, and Rip zoomed into the Hybridrome and were shocked to discover that their fellow racers had already completed their first lap.

"It looks like we have some catching up to do!" said Shu, revving his engine and kicking up snow with his tires.

"Yes! This race isn't over yet!" exclaimed Miguel.

The cars entered the final lap of the race. Francesco and Lightning were battling for the lead.

Lightning and Francesco hurtled toward the finish line. The other racers pushed to catch up.

At the last second, Raoul slipped between the fierce competitors. With inches to spare, he edged out Lightning and Francesco for the win!

Vitaly was proud to award Raoul ÇaRoule the T-ROC Ice Racers Cup. "Congratulations!" he shouted.

"*Merci*, Vitaly," Raoul said happily. "This has been the best T-ROC race yet!"

"And the fun is just beginning," said Lightning. "Who wants to host next?"

RALLY TO THE FINISH!

German superstar racer Max Schnell had invited Lightning McQueen and some of his other international racer friends to the first-ever Black Forest Rally Race Invitational. Lightning was thrilled! He happily accepted the invitation and asked Mater, Luigi, and Guido to go along with him as his race crew.

When Team Lightning arrived in Germany, they were greeted by Max at the airport. *"Willkommen!"* he said.

"Gesundheit," Mater replied. He had changed into his Materhosen on the plane and couldn't wait to show them off. "These here are genuine Materhosen," he told Max. "I can give you the name of my tailor, if you like."

Max smiled at Mater and politely declined his offer.

Team Lightning was soon whisked off to a prerace party.

Lightning was happy to see two more of his international race buddies there: Spanish racer Miguel Camino, and French rally car Raoul ÇaRoule.

While Mater helped serve refreshments, Lightning chatted with Raoul.

"Nice of you to come all this way," Raoul said. "But I will win the race, no?"

"You never know!" said Lightning with a laugh.

At the end of the evening, Lightning told Mater he wanted to head to the Black Forest to practice on the racetrack. An old gentlecar overheard their plans.

"Black Forest at night, eh? Just beware of that *Waldgeister* monster. It's the fastest and scariest monster in the forest."

"A m-m-monster?" Mater said to Lightning. "That sounds bad! Maybe you shouldn't go into that forest, buddy."

The old car chuckled and drove off. "Good luck!" he called over his shoulder.

"I'm sure that 'monster' is just an old legend," said Lightning as he and Mater drove out to the forest.

"I hope yer right," said Mater, relaxing a little. Then he looked at all the surrounding trees. "This place sure is pretty!"

"Especially at top speed!" said Lightning as he revved his engine and took off.

"Whee-hoo! This is fun!" yelled Mater as he raced down a tree-lined path. "I'm happier than a Pinto doing the polka! Last one out of the forest is a rusty tow hitch!"

Following the racetrack, the two best buddies drifted down the fire road, crossed over streams, and cruised across bridges until . . .

they got lost. Lightning had accidentally gone in one direction while Mater had driven off in another.

"Lightning? Lightning? Hellooooo?" yelled Mater.

All Mater could hear was the wind howling and the trees creaking. Suddenly, Mater felt something brush against him.

"*Who's there?*" he gasped as he spun around. A large shadowy figure loomed over him. "The Baldmeister monster! *AHHHHHHH!*" Mater screamed as he took off backward. "He's gonna get me! *AHHHHHH!*"

Meanwhile, Lightning was driving through a different part of the forest. He heard the screaming and headed toward Mater.

"Mater! I'm coming!" he yelled.

Reunited, the two friends found the racetrack and followed it out of the forest.

"The Baldtire monster is *real*," Mater said, shivering.

Lightning sighed. "Mater, you're just imagining things. That monster is not real."

"He *is* real!" Mater insisted. "And I ain't never going back in that forest again!"

The next day was race day! Just before the race began, Mater yelled out to the racers, "You guys aren't still gonna race in the Black Forest, are you?"

"Why wouldn't we?" asked Raoul.

"Because there's a monster that lives in there!" exclaimed Mater.

All the racers grew silent. *"El monstruo?"* said Miguel, wide-eyed.

"There's nothing to worry about," said Lightning. "That monster is just an old legend."

"Okay," said Mater. "Go back into that forest. But don't say I didn't warn ya!"

The green flag dropped. The cars were off!

Lightning navigated down one of the fire roads and then careened around a tricky curve.

Max, Raoul, and Miguel were right on Lightning's bumper as the group broke away from the other racers.

All of a sudden, the racers heard a low grumbling that shook the forest floor. Then Lightning felt something brush his side and heard a creaking sound. "What was that?" he yelled.

The racers stopped in their tracks and looked at each other, panic-stricken.

"Maybe Mater was right," said Lightning. "The *Waldgeister* monster *is* real!"

The racers took off! They sped down a rocky slope and skidded around turns. They saw shadows quickly creeping up behind them. A ravine was just ahead of them. The racers didn't think twice. They raced forward at full speed and leapt over it!

"That monster will not turn me into scrap metal!" yelled Raoul.

"*AHHHHHH!*" they all screamed.

Lightning, Max, Raoul, and Miguel raced for their lives toward the finish line. The fans couldn't believe what they were seeing. All four racers crossed the finish line at the same moment, breaking the Rally Race record for the *fastest time*!

Lightning, Max, Raoul, and Miguel drove up onto the winner's podium. They had all been awarded first place!

"What motivated all of you to race your best today?" asked a reporter.

"Well, we couldn't have done it without the *Waldgeister* monster," said Lightning.

Mater glanced back at the old gentlecar and gave him a wink.

RACING FOR GOOD

*E*arly one morning in Radiator Springs, Lightning McQueen was showing around a very special guest: fellow race car superstar Jeff Gorvette.

"Thanks, Lightning, for helping me put on this race for the Odometer Rollover Foundation," said Jeff.

"My pleasure," said Lightning. "Hopefully we'll sell out the whole stadium tomorrow!"

"That would be awesome! Then we'd be able to provide lots of fuel and tune-ups for older cars," said Jeff.

Lightning and Jeff headed to check out the track.

"Doc would have been happy that we're holding the race at the speedway," Lightning said. "He always wanted to host a charity race here."

"All of our international racing buddies are pretty excited about it, too," said Jeff.

"Speaking of which," said Lightning, "I think I hear one coming now."

It was Francesco Bernoulli, a race car from Italy.

"Ciao, Lightning! Ciao, Jeff!" exclaimed Francesco.

"Ciao to you, Francesco!" Lightning said. "Thanks for coming."

"Of course Francesco is always happy to help out the slower cars. This is because Francesco is so generous and wonderful," the Italian racer said.

Lightning smiled. "You haven't changed one bit, Francesco."

Lightning, Jeff, and Francesco drove inside the speedway. The other racers were already there to check out the track.

Shu Todoroki, the humble yet fierce racer from Japan, rolled down the track toward his friends. Carla Veloso showed off her Latin moves with some quick turns of her wheels. And Nigel Gearsley, the suave and cool English gentlecar, greeted Lightning and Jeff with a wink and a smile.

"Well, mates, care to join us for a few warm-up laps?" Nigel asked.

Lightning was about to answer when a familiar green stock car pulled up. It was Chick Hicks! Lightning was immediately suspicious. Chick was always up to no good.

"A big race without me?" said Chick. "I guess my invitation got lost in the mail."

"Well, Chick, we didn't think this type of race was really your thing," said Jeff.

"I'm a Piston Cup champion! I belong in *every* race!" Chick exclaimed.

Both Jeff and Lightning sighed. They agreed to let Chick participate in the race—as long as he was on his best behavior.

Chick chuckled as the other racers drove off. "Sure, I'll be on my best behavior . . . *after* I beat you all across that finish line!"

Soon the cars were ready to race! They drove up to the starting line, the flag dropped, and they were off!

Francesco quickly took the lead. "Let Francesco show you the meaning of true speed!" he called out.

"Ease up, buddy! This race isn't about winning. It's about helping out Jeff's charity," Lightning said.

"We must still give our fans a good show, no?" said Francesco.

"Of course," Lightning replied.

"So Francesco will be charitable and let Lightning come in second place," Francesco said.

Chick was behind Lightning and Francesco and up to his usual dirty tricks.

"Get outta my way!" he yelled as he bumped into Carla and made Shu spin out.

"Hey, what are you doing?" yelled Nigel.

"What does it look like I'm doing? I'm beating you!" Chick laughed as he zoomed ahead toward Francesco.

In his rearview mirror, Francesco noticed a flash of green. Suddenly, Chick tried to ram Francesco.

Francesco reacted quickly and swerved out of the way. *"Mamma mia!"* he yelled. "Get out of here, you *pazzo* car!"

Chick didn't anticipate Francesco's quick maneuver and ended up crashing into some tires.

Chick managed to catch up to Jeff and Lightning. The two friends winked at each other and slowed down, letting Chick pull out in front.

Chick looked back. "Who's the big winner here today? That's right! It's—"

Taking his eyes off the track made Chick lose control. He went into a tailspin right over the finish line. Chick had won the charity race!

Photographers, reporters, and fans all stared silently as Chick hobbled onto the winner's podium.

"Well, get on with it and give me my prize money and trophy already!" he yelled.

The crowd burst into laughter.

Jeff pulled up next to Chick. "Thanks for helping us raise money for the Odometer Rollover Foundation."

Chick was stunned. "Wait. I did *what*?"

Jeff laughed. "That's right, Chick. You actually raced for a good cause."

As Chick grumbled to himself, Mia and Tia cruised up onto the stage with a big check. They handed it to Jeff.

"On behalf of the Odometer Rollover Foundation, I'd like to thank all the racers who participated in today's charity race," said Jeff.

As Chick drove away, he heard someone call out to him. It was Lizzie.

"Chick! Oh, Chickie! I hear I have you to thank for my next tune-up. How about a kiss?"

"Ugh! I'm outta here!" yelled Chick, and he sped away.

A NEW RACER

It was the first race of the season. Fans cheered as the cars headed toward the finish line. Out in front was number 95, Lightning McQueen. Lightning's friends Bobby Swift, Cal Weathers, and Brick Yardley followed close behind.

With a final burst of speed, Lightning surged past the finish line for the win! "Ka-chow!"

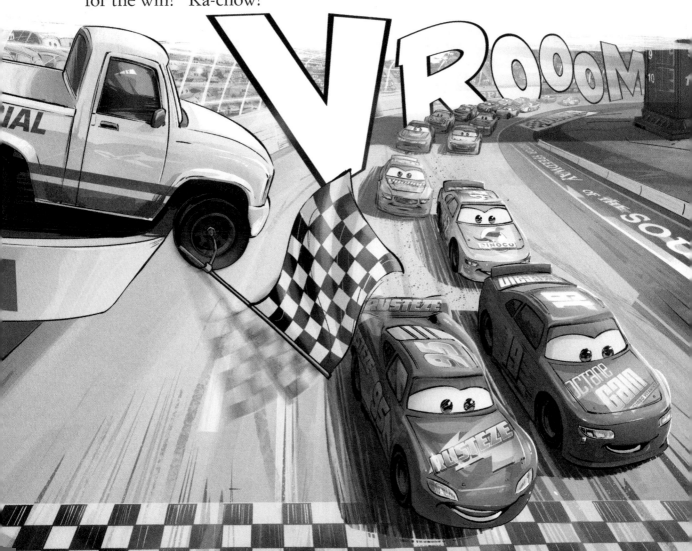

Lightning's season was off to a great start. He kept winning races! Then, at the Motor Speedway of the South, a rookie racer blew past him. The new car's name was Jackson Storm.

After the race, Lightning congratulated Storm on his win.

"Thank you, Mr. McQueen," Storm said. "You have no idea what a pleasure it is for me to finally beat you."

"Thanks!" Lightning said. Then he paused. "Wait. Did you say 'meet,' or '*beat*'?"

Storm smirked. "I think you heard me."

Jackson Storm was part of a new generation of high-tech race cars built to be faster than the cars that had come before. He and the other Next-Gens won race after race!

Soon veteran racers began retiring or losing their sponsors. At the starting line of the final race of the season, Storm mocked Lightning. "Hey, Champ, where'd all your friends go?"

Lightning glared at Storm. He was determined to beat the Next-Gen. But in the last lap of the race, he pushed himself too hard and his tire blew out! As Lightning rolled over and over, his whole world went black.

In the months that followed, Lightning recovered from the crash. He was physically ready to race again, but he wondered if maybe it *was* time to retire.

Lightning thought about his mentor, Doc Hudson. Doc was one of the best racers of his time. But a devastating crash had ended his racing career early.

Lightning made a choice. He wasn't going be pushed out of racing like Doc. He would decide when he was done for himself!

When Lightning told his sponsors, Rusty and Dusty of Rust-eze, that he would race again next season, they were thrilled. They had just made a deal to get Lightning a new training center so he could train on the same equipment as the Next-Gens! But to do it, they had sold Rust-eze to a business car named Sterling.

Sterling greeting Lightning. He was thrilled to meet the race car.

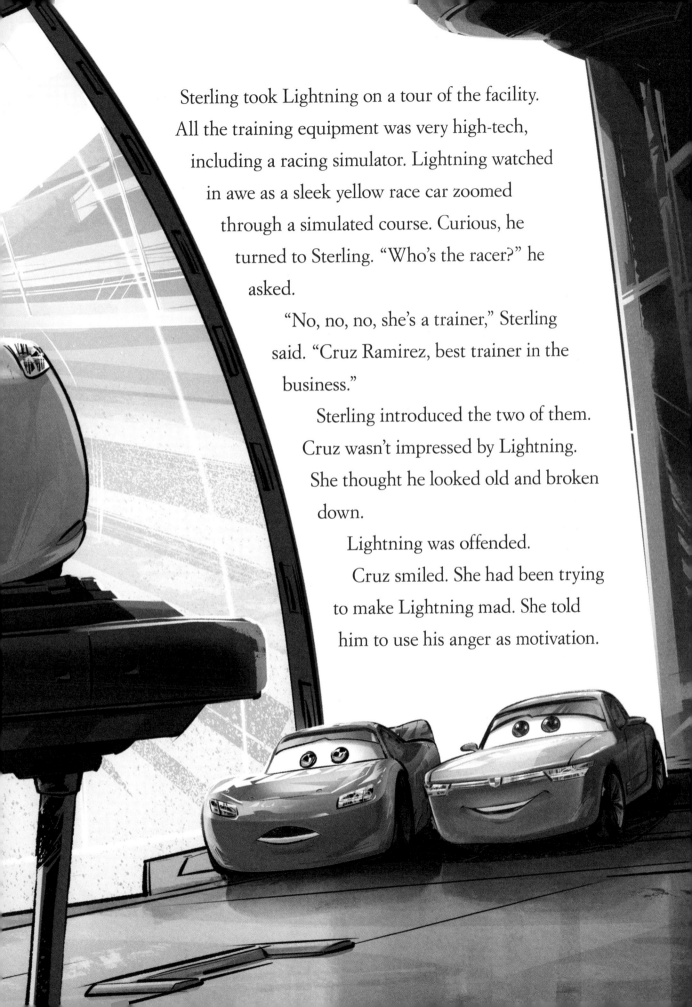

Sterling took Lightning on a tour of the facility. All the training equipment was very high-tech, including a racing simulator. Lightning watched in awe as a sleek yellow race car zoomed through a simulated course. Curious, he turned to Sterling. "Who's the racer?" he asked.

"No, no, no, she's a trainer," Sterling said. "Cruz Ramirez, best trainer in the business."

Sterling introduced the two of them. Cruz wasn't impressed by Lightning. She thought he looked old and broken down.

Lightning was offended.

Cruz smiled. She had been trying to make Lightning mad. She told him to use his anger as motivation.

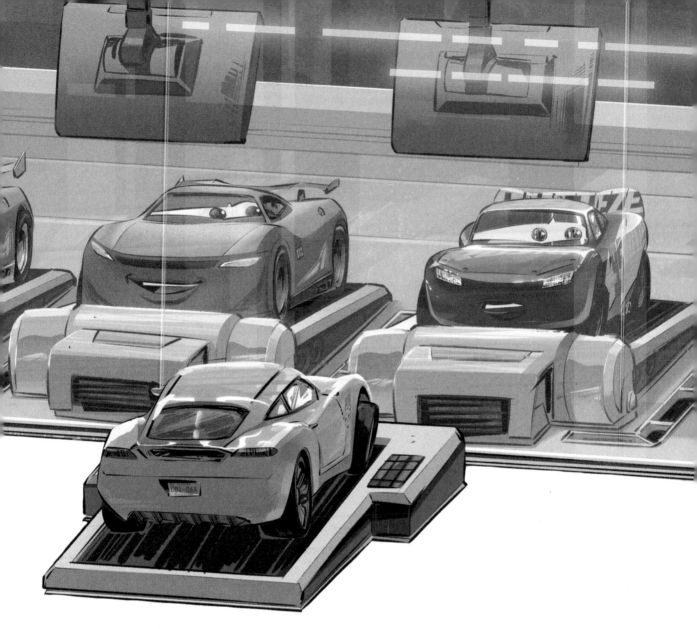

Over the next few weeks, Cruz led Lightning through a series of simple training exercises. She didn't think Lightning was ready for the simulator. Lightning disagreed. He hopped on the simulator—and crashed through its screen!

Sterling thought Lightning's racing career was over. He wanted Lightning to retire and focus on making money for the 95 brand.

Lightning pleaded for one last chance. He was sure he could win if he trained properly. Sterling was skeptical, but finally he agreed—on one condition. If Lightning lost, he'd retire.

Lightning headed to Fireball Beach to restart his training. Cruz went along to track his speed. Lightning thought if he trained on dirt, the same way he had with Doc, he would improve.

Cruz was supposed to be right beside him, tracking his speed, but she was back at the starting line, spinning her wheels. She had never raced on sand before. Lightning gave her some tips. Finally, Cruz managed to race across the beach with Lightning. But Lightning's top speed was still slower than Jackson Storm's.

Lightning decided he needed to train against other racers, so he and Cruz went to the Thunder Hollow Speedway. Lightning disguised himself and signed up for the next race.

It wasn't until the gates closed that Lightning realized that it wasn't a traditional race. It was the Thunder Hollow Crazy Eight demolition derby, where cars smashed into each other. Cruz watched from the infield until the cars came after her, too. Everyone wanted a piece of the newcomers! Cruz was terrified! Lightning shouted racing tips to her and drew the other cars away. At the end of the race, Cruz was declared the winner!

After the race, Lightning lashed out at Cruz. He still hadn't improved his speed, because he was too busy taking care of her. "This is my last chance, Cruz," he shouted. "If I lose, I never get to do this again! If you were a racer, you'd know what I'm talking about. But you're not!"

Cruz turned away. She explained that she had always wanted to be a racer. But in her first race, she had felt out of place. The other cars were bigger and stronger than she was. "When they started their engines, I knew I could never compete. I just left," Cruz said.

Lightning apologized. He hadn't meant to hurt Cruz's feelings.

The next day, Lightning and Cruz went to the famous Thomasville Speedway. Lightning wanted to ask Doc's old crew chief, Smokey, to train him. When they got there, they met Smokey. Three of racing's biggest legends—Junior "Midnight" Moon, River Scott, and Louise "Barnstormer" Nash—were there, too.

Lightning told Smokey that he didn't want to end up the same way Doc had. Smokey led Lightning to his garage. The letters Doc had sent him while he was Lightning's crew chief hung on the wall.

Smokey smiled. "Racing wasn't the best part of Hud's life—you were."

Smokey agreed to train Lightning if he faced the facts—he would never be faster than Storm. But he *could* be smarter than he was. Smokey asked Cruz to stand in as Jackson Storm during Lightning's training. The Legends modified Cruz for racing. She revved her engine and practiced her trash talking.

Smokey trained Lightning the same way he had trained Doc Hudson. The other Legends helped, too. They did sprints and drills. To practice getting through a crowd of racers, Smokey put Lightning and Cruz in a field of stampeding tractors! He was hard on Lightning and challenged him to push himself.

After weeks of training, it was nearly time for the big race. But Smokey had one more test for Lightning—an all-out race against Cruz. The two stayed close together around the track. As they neared the finish line, Lightning gave it everything he had. But it wasn't enough! With a burst of speed, Cruz crossed the line ahead of him. Lightning couldn't believe it. How had he lost?

Finally, the day of the Florida 500 race arrived! Lightning felt nervous as he got into position. His whole racing career was on the line.

The starting flag dropped, and the race began. Smokey and Cruz cheered Lightning on over the headset. Suddenly, Lightning heard Sterling talking to Cruz. He told her to go back to the training center, where she belonged. She was a trainer, not a racer.

Lightning had said the same thing. But he realized he was wrong. Cruz had been awesome on the simulator, on the beach, and on the track at Thomasville. She'd *always* been a racer at heart.

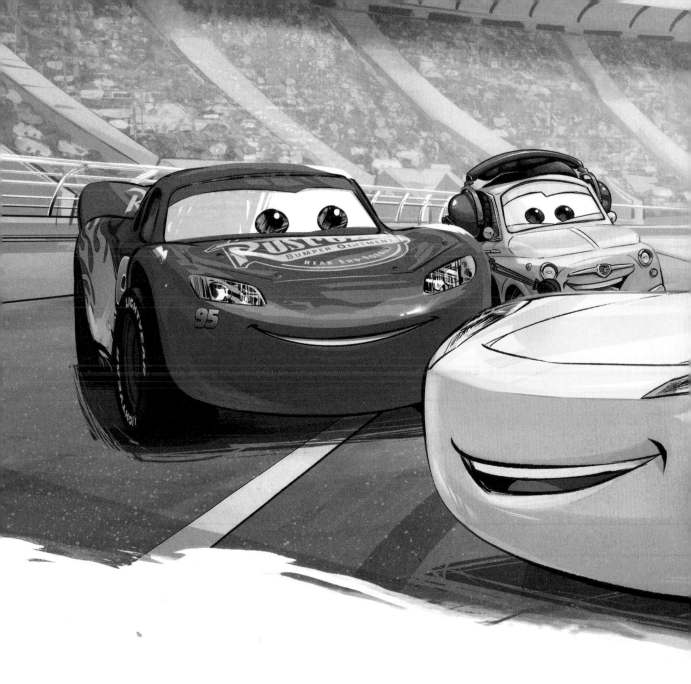

Suddenly, there was a crash right in front of Lightning! He turned
and headed for the pit. Lightning asked Cruz to meet him there. The pit
crew started working on Lightning, but he told them to work on Cruz
instead!

The crew gave Cruz new tires, a paint job—and the number 95. Cruz
was completely confused.

Lightning smiled. He wanted to give her the chance to show the

world that she was a racer. Sterling was furious! But Cruz hit the gas and raced to catch up with the pack.

As Cruz sped around the track, Lightning gave Smokey advice to pass along to Cruz. Finally, Smokey passed Lightning the crew chief headset. Lightning coached Cruz around the track, reminding her of all she had learned. He told her to remember what it was like racing through the herd of tractors. If she saw a gap between cars, she had to take it!

Cruz saw an opening and shot through! The crowd began cheering for the new 95! With only a few laps left, Cruz moved up until she was just one car behind the leader—Jackson Storm!

Storm dropped back to taunt Cruz. He didn't think she deserved to be in the race. She would never be a racer.

Storm's words hit Cruz hard and she slowed down, falling behind Storm. But Lightning wasn't about to let Cruz lose. He knew that Storm was just scared of her. Lightning urged her on. He believed she could win.